THE HIDDEN

Kelderan Runic Warriors #5

JESSIE DONOVAN

Mythical Lake Press, LLC

This book is a work of fiction. Names, characters, places, and incidents are either the product of the writer's imagination or are used fictitiously, and any resemblance to actual persons, living or dead, business establishments, events, or locales is entirely coincidental.

The Hidden
Copyright © 2019 Laura Hoak-Kagey
Mythical Lake Press, LLC
First Print Edition

Cover Art by Laura Hoak-Kagey of Mythical Lake Design
ISBN: 978-1944776244

Books by Jessie Donovan

Love in Scotland

Crazy Scottish Love (LiS #1)

Chaotic Scottish Wedding (LiS #2)

Asylums for Magical Threats

Blaze of Secrets (AMT #1)

Frozen Desires (AMT #2)

Shadow of Temptation (AMT #3)

Flare of Promise (AMT #4)

Cascade Shifters

Convincing the Cougar (CS #0.5)

Reclaiming the Wolf (CS #1)

Cougar's First Christmas (CS #2)

Resisting the Cougar (CS #3)

Kelderan Runic Warriors

The Conquest (KRW #1)

The Barren (KRW #2)

The Heir (KRW #3)

The Forbidden (KRW #4)

The Hidden (KRW #5)

The Survivor (KRW #6)

Treasured by the Dragon (SD #13)

Stonefire Dragons Universe

Winning Skyhunter (SDU #1)

Transforming Snowridge (SDU #2)

Tahoe Dragon Mates

The Dragon's Choice (TDM #1)

The Dragon's Need (TDM #2)

The Dragon's Bidder (TDM #3)

The Dragon's Charge (TDM #4)

Chapter One

Vala walked up to her lord, placed her hands on his bare, light blue shoulders, and kneaded the knotted flesh. Thorin leaned back into her touch and groaned. "Your fingers will distract me, zyla."

"Good, then I'll achieve my goal." Digging her fingers in deeper, she added, "You shouldn't worry about tomorrow's first open meeting with other half-Brevkan individuals inside the Kelderan colony on Jasvar. Not only have you gone over every detail ten times, several people have confirmed they will be there. I know it will be a successful first step in bringing everyone out into the open."

Thorin shook his head. "Just because they confirmed doesn't mean they'll show up. After all, once everyone in the Kelderan colony knows their true identities, there's no going back to anonymity."

She pressed her fingers even deeper into Thorin's

skin, and he let out a low moan. She resisted a smile as she said, "While that may be, you made your true identity public weeks ago and few have sneered or made comments about your parentage."

Her lord, Thorin Jarrell, was originally from the planet Keldera like her, but his father had been a Brevkan warrior. The Brevkan had been—and still were—the most hated enemies of Kelderans. More than twenty years ago the war between the two worlds had ended and left many Kelderans with decimated families. To say they held grudges was an understatement. She wouldn't put it past many of them to want vengeance on anything remotely tied to the Brevkan. The hatred back home was part of the reason she and Thorin were on the planet Jasvar, as members of a new Kelderan colony.

The other reason was for a fresh start for a Barren like her, to be with the half-Brevkan male she loved. Both outcasts in their own way, they'd found their soul mate in each other and were determined to make a new life together.

Her husband placed a hand over one of hers and she stopped moving her fingers. Meeting her gaze, he said, "Most of those who attend the meeting probably won't be warriors who can pin and restrain another male within the blink of an eye, zyla. They have reason to worry, especially if they have families to protect."

Vala knew her lord well enough to know words

wouldn't work right now. If he didn't relax and get some sleep, he wouldn't be at his best at the meeting. While she loved him regardless of his charm and temper levels, more than a few people would run away at an angry look from Thorin Jarrell, a former general in the Kelderan Army.

And so she would try another tactic. Brushing his short, black hair at his temple, she smiled at her husband. "You know, the more you call me zyla, the more I want you all to myself."

Thorin turned and stood, pulling her against his chest. "I sense this is a tactic. But I can never resist you, zyla."

The Kelderan term of endearment was almost always used by lords for their brides; it meant dear one or beloved. Vala decided to use the masculine equivalent. "That's good, because I never want you to, zylar."

With a growl, Thorin lowered his head and kissed her.

The second his tongue entered her mouth, licking and tangling as if he would die without her, Vala forgot about everything else but her lord. The male she never thought she'd have, the one who didn't care that she was one of the Barren and unable to give him a child, was her world and her future now.

She loved him more than life itself, and he felt the same about her.

So when he ran a hand down her side and then

her leg to lift it, she pressed her core against his already hard cock, rubbing and letting him know she was more than ready for him.

With a growl, Thorin grabbed her rear and rocked her against him. She couldn't help but groan at the delicious friction of her nipples against his hard chest.

Thorin broke the kiss. She barely noticed his glowing blue eyes—one of the traits he'd inherited from his Brevkan half—as he murmured, "I don't care if this is a distraction. I want you. I need you." He kissed her roughly. "Tell me you have the time."

It was hard to think with Thorin's hard muscles pressed up against her front, but she managed, "I cleared my schedule, knowing you would probably want me this evening."

He growled. "I'm still unsure about how I'm worthy of you."

She stroked the side of his face. "Let's not debate this again. Kiss me, Thorin, and claim me as your own."

Stepping back, he tugged off first her skirt and then her top. His gaze roamed her body, heat building with each second, to the point her nipples ached.

With a growl, Thorin shimmied out of the tight warrior pants he still wore despite him no longer being in the army, and tossed them aside. At the predatory look in his eyes, she shivered in a good way.

He scooped her up and gently laid her on the bed. His hands went from her shoulders to her ribcage, then her waist, and finally down her legs. His rough, warm skin against hers made her wet between the thighs.

His hands wrapped around her ankles, but instead of spreading her legs, he lifted one to his face and murmured, "The red band around your calf. It's almost gone."

The band had appeared shortly after he'd claimed her as his possession—the person a Brevkan male instinctually recognizes as their own. "I know, but I have no idea why."

As he stared at it some more, Vala knew she'd have to entice him a little. Otherwise, he'd ponder if the band was related to his Brevkan heritage and if the fading meant something would happen to her.

And since they didn't know enough about her husband's paternal heritage, they might never find the answer.

No, it was best to make her lord forget all about the faded red band on her skin.

Moving a hand to one of her nipples, Vala rolled and tugged. At her moan, Thorin's gaze zeroed in on her fingers. She said, "Please, Thorin. Forget about that for now and claim me."

She continued teasing her tight bud, already

feeling the pressure building. Thorin moved to her other nipple, drew it into his mouth, and suckled.

While she was called strong by many, Vala had no difficulty giving Thorin control. She whimpered as he lightly bit her. "Zylar, I'm so close."

His fingers found her other nipple, and between his mouth and his hand, Vala cried out as wave after wave of pleasure coursed through her body, making her arch her back into her lord's touch.

She'd barely come down from her high when Thorin placed his cock at her entrance, teased her a few times, and thrust to the hilt. He brought his face down to hers, his hot breath dancing across her lips as he said, "I love you, Vala."

"Then show me, zylar. And don't you dare hold back."

Even though he didn't need her permission, Thorin was constantly afraid his rough lovemaking would break her. So at her words, he finally let go, moving his hips as his skin glowed a light purple— another Brevkan trait.

He increased his movements, taking her lips as he thrust hard, moving the bed with his actions. Each pump of his hips made her dig her nails deeper into his skin, just the way he liked.

Thorin finally stilled and growled into her mouth. His skin glowed even brighter as he came.

The oddly addictive scent only she would smell filled her nostrils, and she scratched her nails down his back and wrapped her legs around her male. Since she'd spent most of her life thinking she'd always be alone, she cherished him being inside her and always wanted him to know she accepted all of him.

When Thorin finally slumped on top of her, Vala hugged him close. She loved the solidness of his weight. He was strong and powerful, and yet he'd never hurt her.

He was her protector, her lover, her best friend, her everything.

Thorin finally rolled over, taking her with him. Laying her head on his chest, she listened to his heartbeat a few seconds before murmuring, "I think we should go again."

Her lord's deep voice filled her ears. "When did the band start fading, Vala? You must've done a good job distracting me if I hadn't noticed it until now."

Leave it to Thorin to remember that detail so soon after an orgasm. And knowing him as she did, he wouldn't fall for another seduction attempt so soon. No, he wanted answers and wouldn't stop until he had them.

With a sigh, she replied, "I don't know exactly. Two weeks, maybe a month? Since I wear trousers to all my self-defense sessions with the human females, I don't look at it that often anymore."

He gripped her hip possessively. "Is there pain? Warmth? Tell me everything you know."

"I'm sure it's nothing, Thorin. I don't feel any different." He grunted and she added, "I don't. If you think I'm going to lie to you, then you aren't the male I thought you were."

Placing a finger under her chin, he raised her head gently until she met his gaze. "I just want to make sure it's nothing to worry about. I can't lose you, zyla. I just can't."

Some might think his words were hyperbolic, but Vala knew they weren't. Thorin had spent nearly thirty years trying to control his rages, which were sudden bursts of negative emotions and horrific visions filled with blood. They were all due to his Brevkan half, and he'd been close to a breaking point when they'd first met.

However, ever since meeting and claiming her, Thorin had been stable and nearly nightmare and vision-free. If something happened to her, she was afraid he might fall into a rage and never come out of it again.

And if that happened, the leaders of the colony would have no choice but to kill him.

Hugging him closer to her, she said, "If something was wrong, I would tell you. But it's the truth—I feel no different than last week or the weeks before that. Besides, for all we know, the band is a temporary signal to other Brevkan that a female has been claimed and could already be pregnant."

Not that Vala ever would be. A genetic test as a

baby had verified her infertility, which had resulted in her being shipped off to the Barren and given a tattoo on her forehead for everyone to know what she was.

Thorin grunted. "Maybe. If anyone shows up at the meeting tomorrow, I'm going to make it one of the first things I ask about."

She rolled her eyes. "There are more important things to discuss first. Maybe see if anyone is close to the breaking point of not being able to control a rage. Or, try to see if others know a male with Brevkan DNA can paralyze a female with his post-orgasm musk if she is meant to be his possession. There are so many important things that need to be shared. The band around my leg isn't worth mentioning."

"I would disagree again, but I know we'll just go around in circles. And I have a better way to spend our time."

Thorin's hand lightly stroked between her thighs as she feigned innocence. "Oh, is that so? I wonder what that could be."

"Since when do you play coy, Vala Yarlen?" He rolled her onto her back and pinned her hands above her head. "I think it's time to claim you in one of your favorite ways."

She resisted a smile. "And what way would that be? I may have forgotten."

His fingers danced between her thighs again, and

she sucked in a breath. Thorin's gravelly voice caressed her body as he said, "Then let me remind you."

Keeping her hands pinned over her head, he quickly slid into her and stared into her eyes as he moved his hips in slow, deliberate movements. Soon his free hand was doing naughty things to her nipples, and Vala forgot about everything but the male she loved above her.

Chapter Two

Thorin woke instantly when Vala rolled off the mattress, picked up the basket next to their bed containing the glowing organisms used for low lighting on Jasvar, and made her way toward the cleansing room.

Not that her waking up in the middle of the night was unusual. No, he was merely attuned to her every movement in his presence. In part because of his warrior training, but also because he still had trouble believing she was his bride.

After all, shrugging off decades of feeling lesser for his mixed heritage wasn't as easy as he wished.

Then he heard Vala gasp, and he was up and at the door in seconds. "What's wrong, Vala?"

"N-Nothing."

At the tremble in her voice, he growled. "You're lying. Tell me, or I'll break down this door."

A second later, her soft reply came. "It's unlocked."

Thorin didn't hesitate to enter. Vala stood against the wall, staring at the closed toilet lid in disbelief. His first instinct was to find the threat and eliminate it. "What did you see? Is it one of the snakes? Or the spiders? Let me know, and I'll plan my attack."

The fauna on Jasvar was often deadly if one didn't approach the situation carefully.

Vala shook her head, keeping her gaze averted. "It's not that."

He closed the distance between them. As he lightly lifted her chin, he softened his voice. "Talk to me, zyla. I can't help you if I don't know what's wrong."

When her eyes met his, there was a mixture of fear and confusion. If the lighting were stronger, the markings on her body would be the colors of yellow and white to match.

She swallowed, and Thorin's gut clenched. His first thought was that he'd been too rough with her and had hurt her in some way. "Are you in pain?"

"No."

Stroking her cheek with his thumb, he relied on his warrior's training to keep his voice calm and his emotions in check. "Then what has you so terrified, zyla?"

She searched his eyes for a few beats, and each second made his stomach knot. Vala was the most important person in his life. He couldn't lose her, no matter what. But if he had hurt her and she was trying to placate his feeling, he just might.

Vala swallowed and then whispered, "There was blood."

Shame descended on him, making his heart and lungs constrict. "I'm so sorry. I'll fetch the doctor and I will never be rough again. I promise not to touch you until you wish it."

As he moved to walk away, battling the urge to lash out at himself, Vala gripped his wrist. "No, I'm not in pain. It's not because of you."

He met her gaze again, trying his best to keep his composure. "It must be because of me. You have no monthly courses because of your genetic birth condition."

"You're right, I never did. But I think I do now."

He frowned. "You're not making sense, Vala. And you usually always do."

She tightened her fingers around his arm. "I know I'm not, and I'm confused as you are. But I think I should see a doctor."

Desperate to do anything to help erase his bride's fears, Thorin nodded. "I'll go at once."

She shook her head. "No, no, don't worry about it right now. It can wait until morning."

"And let you stew in fear until then? I think not. I will return as soon as possible with Iljan."

Iljan was the head doctor inside the Kelderan

colony on Jasvar. One who had a small, often sickly child. If Thorin gave Vala a chance, she'd say not to disturb Iljan since the doctor's daughter was ill yet again.

However, he couldn't risk his bride's health. Iljan knew middle of the night calls were part of his job description.

Before Vala could ask him to stay, Thorin gently removed her fingers and exited first the room and then their shared apartment.

As he walked down the winding corridors, he tried his best to keep his fear at bay. He suspected his bride was trying to shield him, in an effort to control his rages. However, he wouldn't be kept in the dark. He'd ensure the doctor gave him a full report on why Vala was bleeding.

It was most likely because of him, and he'd do whatever it took to beg her forgiveness and ensure it never happened again. Reining in his Brevkan side was never easy, but he'd have to find a way to erase it somehow. That may be the only way to keep Vala as his bride.

And he needed to keep her near. She'd shone some light into his life and Thorin didn't think he could go back to living alone in the darkness.

As Vala waited for the doctor, her mind buzzed with what had happened.

What she hadn't told Thorin was that her lower belly twisted in knots, too. Combined with the blood and the tenderness of her breasts the past few days, it was as others had described monthly courses to her.

Which was impossible. Vala was unable to have them.

Maybe it was something else. Not that the thought made her any calmer. Even putting aside how Thorin wouldn't survive her death, Vala had no desire to die. For the first time since she was a child, she was truly happy. Not just because she'd found love, but also because she was finally allowed to be herself and not live in constant shame of her birth defect. She even had a role within the Kelderan colony, to help with educating the Jasvarians about her people.

She was valued as an equal, which was something she'd never known back on Keldera.

And after everything she'd endured in her early life, fate couldn't be cruel enough to snatch away her happiness via some sort of incurable condition.

By the time the doctor came and banished Thorin from the apartment to conduct his scans and examination, Vala did her best to push every thought from her mind. She'd save her worry for later, if it were needed.

However, as the doctor used a portable body

scanner over her midsection, he frowned. "That can't be right." He fiddled with the device and scanned her again.

Wanting to know what was going on, she asked, "What's wrong, Doctor?"

Iljan was no more than an acquaintance, a male she'd only met after moving to Jasvar to become part of the Kelderan colony. However, unlike many of the doctors she'd worked with back on Keldera, Iljan didn't dismiss her or view her as an annoyance. He'd always been fair, and more importantly, truthful with her.

The male finally met her gaze. "On the way here, I quickly accessed your digital records to ensure I knew about your health history. However, what I read and what I'm seeing now are two different things."

Vala sat up and laid her hands in her lap, careful to keep them away from the area giving the male such concern. "I can handle the truth, Doctor. No matter how extreme it is, please tell me what concerns you."

His steady gaze soothed her nerves a bit. "To put it concisely, you were born with a severely misshapen uterus. It's the reason you were given to the Barren, and why you never had a monthly cycle. However, this scan shows a perfectly normal-looking one. It makes no sense."

She blinked at the last part. She may be no

doctor, but internal organs didn't shift and change on their own. "Pardon?"

"I have a spare scanner in my bag. Let me try again."

As she watched the doctor move across the room, her gaze fell on the fading red band on her leg.

A thought instantly came to her, one that was ridiculous. Strong as her husband may be, not even he could will her body to right itself.

However, a niggle of doubt crept into her mind, one that had always been there. If a Brevkan's need to claim a possession was instinct and fate, Vala should never have triggered the reaction with Thorin. From what little they knew of the Brevkan, lineage was important to them. So much so their biology often focused on the act of procreation, dismissing desires, love, or even a willingness.

After all, Thorin's mother had been raped by a Brevkan warrior, his instinct not caring about the young woman or her wishes.

And yet, Vala had reacted to Thorin's post-orgasm musk, triggering the need to claim her or leave her paralyzed for life.

Maybe, just maybe, the Brevkan male biology had a way of correcting things to ensure a continuance of the line.

Fear flooded her body and she gripped the sheets. Some may be happy with the news, but it terrified her. The one thing Thorin never wanted was children of his own. And since no matter of birth control had seemed to prevent conception during the Brevkan wars, if Vala could conceive, then it would happen.

The doctor returned, and she did her best to stare at her fingers clenching the sheets. Never in her life did she hope for a mistake as she did for the initial scanning.

But when the doctor blew out a breath, her insides twisted further. His words didn't help, either. "The same result. If you're able to move without pain, I'd like to take you to the hospital to examine you further."

She finally met his eyes, an act she never would've been allowed to do back on her old planet of Keldera. "I will on one condition."

Iljan raised an eyebrow. "Which is?"

"Don't tell Thorin what's going on. Let me be the one to do it, once we know for sure."

The doctor tucked the medical scanner into his doctor's bag. "Legally, males still have the right to know everything about their brides under Kelderan law."

"But we're on Jasvar. I wouldn't be talking to you right now if we weren't."

He met her eyes again at that. "Fair point. However, I promised your lord a full report. If you don't give it to him immediately after I finish the examination inside the hospital, then I will do so. I made the promise with him first."

She bobbed her head. "I understand, and will tell him quickly, as soon as we're alone."

Because the news could provoke a rage, and Vala would be the only thing to keep him calm.

Or, she still hoped her presence would. If it proved true that her body was changing and she'd be able to bear children, it meant Thorin would either have to accept it or never touch her again.

And the last thing she ever wanted was for him to resent her by giving her a child and forever looking at both her and the little boy or girl with disdain.

No. She couldn't start thinking the worst until she had all the facts. The initial appearance of blood and the doctor's words had thrown her off guard. Now, however, she had time to gather her thoughts and remain calm. She would never use emotions to manipulate Thorin, and tears would most likely do it.

In order for even the slightest chance of keeping her lord, she had to be strong. And logical. And everything else people expected of her.

True, she'd probably not be able to hide the truth from her friend Kalahn since the Kelderan princess often picked up stray thoughts via telepathy, but to everyone else, she had to.

THORIN PACED the hallway so aggressively he would've started a small trench if it'd been dirt instead of the synthetic compound used for all the initial Kelderan apartment buildings on Jasvar.

He should be with Vala, holding her hand, and giving her whatever strength he could. Not banished to the hall, unable to lend her his love and hear the truth of whatever was wrong with her.

Although if his suspicions were correct, he couldn't blame his bride for not wanting him by her side.

Thorin clenched the fingers of one hand into a fist and eyed the wall. It was tempting to hit it repeatedly until he bruised and bloodied his hand. It wasn't enough of a punishment for hurting his female, but it would at least be a start.

The door opened and he whirled around, his eyes searching first the doctor's and then Vala's. "What's wrong with Vala?"

Iljan glanced at Vala and then answered, "I need to run more tests. If you could help Vala to the hospital, I'll race ahead to get everything set up."

The doctor took a step, but Vala spoke before he could move further. "Please tell my lord that he didn't hurt me. Thorin won't believe me, no matter how many times I say it."

Iljan looked at Vala, and then Thorin, his brows furrowed. "Most definitely not. It's—never mind. You didn't injure her, Thorin. That I vow."

Kelderan vows were serious, and he had no choice but to believe the other male.

Of course Iljan's evasiveness only heightened his unease and worry.

The doctor jogged away before anyone could ask more questions and Thorin searched Vala's black eyes. His guilt faded a fraction, but he refused to let it dissipate completely. "There is something you're not telling me, zyla. Please, I need to know what's wrong."

She closed the distance between them and placed one hand on his chest and the other on his jaw. "Let the doctor run his tests first. I don't want to worry you unnecessarily."

As she stroked his skin, he leaned into her touch. "I will worry regardless."

She smiled and stood on her tiptoes to kiss him briefly. "I love you, Thorin Jarrell. Please trust me on this. Once I have all the facts, then we'll talk."

Trust had never been easy for him, and even now with his bride, he wanted to keep pushing until he had all the information.

But as she stroked his chest and stared up at him with love in her eyes, he nodded. "I trust you." He kissed her gently before scooping her into his arms.

Vala squeaked. "I can walk, Thorin."

"I may trust you and will wait to discuss what's going on. However, if you think I'm going to let you walk on your own when there could be something wrong with you, then you don't know me at all."

Looping her arms around his neck, she laid her head on his shoulder. "I do know you, zylar. Better than anyone."

Something about her words and tone made him uneasy, but he pushed it aside. All that mattered was conveying his bride to the hospital as quickly and gently as he could. The sooner he got there, the sooner he could find out what was going on with his love.

Chapter Three

Two hours and numerous tests later, Vala sat and waited for the doctor to speak. He'd been studying the latest results for a full two minutes.

Only because she'd worked with doctors over the years back on Keldera, when it came to children or epidemics, did she hold her tongue. She'd seen many a parent push and bully a doctor for an answer, which only made revealing the result take that much longer.

With a grunt, Iljan set aside his precious notescreen—Jasvar was a low-tech planet and every Kelderan treasured what technology they'd been able to bring with them—and finally spoke. "The initial results from the first scan haven't changed. Your uterus is now healthy and functional, as are your ovaries. The blood is from the first shedding of your inner uterine lining. While I can't guarantee anything, my initial diagnosis is that you're no longer barren. If you wish, you should be able to have a child."

Vala had been preparing herself for that answer, to the point she was able to ask calmly, "Do you know why the change happened?"

He shook his head. "That I can't determine. It could be something you've eaten on Jasvar or even some sort of microbe on this planet that heals and restores flesh. But at the moment, I can't say. If you'll occasionally allow more testing and interviews with me, then I might be able to better pinpoint the cause. Because if I could discover it, we could help any female who wishes to have children and can't, thus allowing them to live without stigma."

The sincerity of Iljan's words didn't go unnoticed. "Someone you know was or is labeled a Barren."

Iljan grimaced. "Or, could be one day—my daughter."

The reason why such a young, well-liked doctor had made the journey to Jasvar, where he might soon have to practice medical techniques from hundreds of years in the past if their technology faded, made sense. On Jasvar, the Barren weren't kept separate from the rest of Kelderan society as they were back on their home world.

Maybe before Iljan's revelation, she could've allowed him to think it had to do with being on a new planet with a multitude of new organisms.

However, her gut knew it was because of Thorin, and Iljan should know the truth. Especially since her lord had come forward publicly about his mixed heritage some weeks ago, it wasn't a betrayal to bring it up. Taking a deep breath, she spoke before she lost her nerve. "Or, it may have something to do with my lord's heritage."

Iljan raised his brows. "There is much we don't know about the Brevkan, but I've never heard of them being able to heal or repair bodies to such an extent."

Neither had she. However, she explained about the red band, how it had faded over time, and even revealed her early paralysis, when she'd first been affected by Thorin and how it signaled a possession. When she finished, she added, "All of it seems too coincidental to be unconnected."

Iljan had sat down by this point, and he crossed his arms over his chest. "I never rule something out until I can scientifically prove otherwise, but that does seem a stretch. The only way to see if your hypothesis is valid or not is to take fluid samples from your lord and run more tests. And forgive me, Vala, but until you talk with him, I can't do that. He has to know why I'm running the tests. The colony charter is clear about transparency."

Kason tro el Vallen—a prince from Keldera who now helped run the Kelderan colony on Jasvar—had wanted to prevent secrecy as much as possible. Not being as forthright as the government and the royal family could have been had stirred a lot of trouble back on Keldera, to the point it had nearly cost the Kelderan king his life.

She admired the charter's ambitions, of course, but Thorin hated his Brevkan half. So much so, he had declined any and all tests since they'd moved to the colony on Jasvar.

And after she told her lord about the doctor's findings, she didn't know what to expect. Coaxing him to allow testing may not be possible.

However, she wouldn't know until she tried. With a sigh, she bobbed her head. "I understand. If I could have some time alone with Thorin, I'll see if he will agree to the tests."

Iljan searched her gaze. "If you need me here, I can stay."

"No, no, that's not necessary. Go look after your daughter. She needs you more than I do right now."

He hesitated, but finally stood. "Call the nurse if you need me to come back, and I'll return as quickly as I can. I live on the floor above the hospital, so not far."

"Thank you, Doctor. Tell Thorin to come in on your way out, please."

After one more glance, Iljan exited the room.

Thorin waltzed into the room within seconds, taking her hands and squeezing them lightly. "What did he say?"

Staring into Thorin's eyes, she took a moment to memorize the love mixed with concern. Because once she told him that she could have children now, she had no idea how he would react or look at her in the future.

And if it were with disgust or disappointment, Vala's heart would break into a thousand pieces.

THE SECOND he was alone with his bride, Thorin took Vala's hands in his and tried his best not to worry about the flashing colors of her markings. She was nervous, as well as a little bit afraid.

So he asked what the doctor said, and after a few seconds, Vala took a deep breath and answered, "Somehow, my body has healed itself and the blood was a sign of my first monthly course. I am no longer barren, zylar. Going forward, I can have children."

He stared, unable to respond despite the multitude of questions swirling inside his head. Not even the advanced Kelderan technologies could repair inner organs to such a degree, to help someone like Vala.

But somehow, some way, she could have children now.

Children that would be part Brevkan and sentenced to a life of inner demons and constantly fighting rages that wanted to come to the surface.

All the things he had endured, things he'd never wanted another to suffer the same way.

Vala's voice cut through his mental haze. "Please tell me what you're thinking, Thorin. The silence only makes it worse."

He hadn't realized that he'd released Vala's hands and started pacing. Turning toward her again, the sight of fear in her eyes went straight to his heart. He needed to soothe his bride. Closing the distance, he pulled her against his chest.

Vala was his everything. No matter his fears, he needed to talk with her and figure out a solution. Because life without his bride wasn't worth living. "I'm sorry, zyla. I'm here, and we'll figure this out together."

She lightly stroked his chest. "Will we, though? I know you don't want children."

As much as it pained him to ask—Vala's answer could make him face his worst fears—he did. "But do you want children of your own instead of adopting?"

"Maybe at one time I thought so, when I was younger and only wished to be considered normal instead of an outcast. However, in the present, all I want is you, Thorin. You loved me as I was, accepted me as I was, and I can't imagine my life without you."

He hugged her tighter against his chest, treasuring the female he didn't deserve. However, his sense of relief was short-lived. Wetness trailed down his chest, meaning his female was probably crying.

Gently maneuvering her face to look at him, the sadness and desperation he saw there stole his breath away. "I'm right here, love. There are plenty of ways to prevent pregnancies. We can try any and all of them."

A sob escaped her throat, putting his every nerve on end. Something was wrong. Something Vala wasn't telling him.

He lightly stroked her cheek and murmured, "Talk to me, Vala. I can't help if I don't know all the facts."

She sniffled a few times before her low voice filled the room. "I'm fairly sure that no matter what we try, it won't matter."

"You're not making sense."

"I know. But Thorin, I think the reason my body healed itself is because of you." He frowned in confusion, but she continued before he could say anything. "Remember the red band around my ankle and how it started to fade? I think it's a signal, one that I've been claimed but not yet impregnated by a Brevkan. As it lightens, it signals I'm closer to breeding, as they put it. Somehow, someway, I think your semen has healing chemicals, ones that ensure a female can continue the line."

He wanted to deny it outright. But damn it, he knew so little about his father's people.

Vala spoke again. "And if I'm correct, it means no matter what we do, eventually I'll be with child.

Not through any choice of yours or mine, but it will simply happen."

At that, Vala sobbed and crashed against his chest.

Her distress cut through his shock, and he rubbed circles on her back and kissed her hair. In that moment, all that mattered was his female.

As he continued to hold her and murmur sweet nothings, a different section of Thorin's brain tried to process everything. If Vala were correct that no matter what happened, she would one day fall pregnant, it meant he could either never touch her again or embrace one of his greatest fears—passing on the monster-like genes of his rapist father.

The thought of giving up Vala forever sent a resounding no through his mind. He had promised to always love her, cherish her, and protect her. And he meant it.

Although he wasn't as sure about himself when it came to holding a child of his in the future, though. Simply giving a baby life would sentence it to an existence of pain and suffering. All because he was the father.

What he needed was more information. He'd already met one half-Brevkan male who'd fathered children. Maybe there were others. And maybe, just maybe, if they all met and shared information, they could discover a way to prevent as much—or maybe even all—of the suffering associated with a part Brevkan individual's upbringing.

"Thorin."

At the exhaustion in his bride's voice, he focused all of his attention on her. Cupping her cheek with one of his hands, he kissed her gently and said, "I love you, zyla. And don't worry, I'm not going anywhere."

She searched his gaze. "But it's the one thing you never wanted. Can you really live with it?"

"For you, anything."

"I want to believe you, but it can't be that simple."

"Yes, it can. You brought lightness into my life when I thought I'd never have it. Not to mention a happiness I've never known. I would even give my life to save yours, Vala. I can do this, too." She opened her mouth, but he beat her to it. "I have a plan, my lovely bride. One that will require your help."

Her brows came together. "A plan about what?"

"Rather than passively wait for other part Brevkan individuals to come forward, we're going to search them out. What I need is information, especially about any of their children. Together, we might be able to minimize any suffering. And if I can do that, then it will be easier for me to accept and not feel guilty about having a child."

"Thorin," she murmured.

"We'll do this together, love. As soon as you feel up to it."

Wiping her eyes, she stood a little taller. "All I need is a nap, and then I'll be ready."

He smoothed back a stray hair from her face. "No, you should take a few days to rest first."

She raised an eyebrow. "Will you wait?"

"No," he said sheepishly.

"Exactly. We're going to do this together, Thorin. Which also means I need you to do something. The doctor wants to run tests to confirm my suspicions. I know you've avoided it, but now…"

"But now, it could help any child of ours," he finished.

She bobbed her head. "So will you do it?"

The thought of scanners and needles made his skin crawl, but he'd suffered worse things in his life. "I will." Scooping her up, he held her protectively against his chest. "But first, I'll take you home to rest. And just know that no amount of arguing will change my mind about that."

Vala smiled, and it helped ease his nerves. Yes, for the beautiful female in his arms, he would truly do anything.

And that included facing his greatest fear of fathering a part Brevkan child.

Chapter Four

T he next day, once Thorin had ensured Vala
was asleep with her friend Kalahn to watch
over her, Thorin left their apartment and headed to
the small meeting space inside the colony's living
area.

While he fully intended to search out other part-
Brevkan individuals, he'd promised Vala they'd do it
together and he needed to wait for his bride to regain
her strength. However, he could still attend the
prescheduled meeting as planned. He doubted he'd
be lucky enough to meet any fathers or mothers
there, but he would go all the same.

As usually happened, with each step away from
his bride, Thorin's skin warmed and his brain grew
restless. It was the cue for him to fall back on
rhythmic breathing and imagine his bride smiling at

him. The combination had yet to fail him so far when it came to preventing his rages.

He hadn't had one for months and he wasn't about to let them return now. While the idea of becoming a father was foreign to him, to the degree it felt as if he walked in a dream, he wouldn't endanger any child. And to ensure that, he had to be certain he could remain calm under any and all circumstances.

Approaching the plain, gray composite door, Thorin entered the meeting room and paused. Even though he was a few minutes early, ten individuals sat inside the space.

He noticed none of them sat next to one another, plus the room was silent. However, their presence was most definitely an accomplishment. And ten attendees may be a high enough number to find a parent among them.

Thorin walked to the front of the room and stood behind the simple podium. All eyes looked at him, but after being in the Kelderan Army for so many years—often in a leadership role—the attention didn't bother him.

He glanced at the individuals, a mixed group of males and females. Some had Kelderan skin tones, and others had Brevkan ones that had probably relied on heavy cosmetics for most of their lives to hide it. Thorin finally spoke. "I honestly didn't expect anyone to attend. However, I'm grateful for your courage. Coming forward almost guarantees you will never return to Keldera. At least, not until the laws are changed substantially."

A male with light blue skin similar to Thorin's spoke up. "Given the freedoms we're allowed here, I don't think any of us would return. Much like your bride."

Thorin hadn't met the male before. He must've researched Thorin before attending. "As I'm sure each of you understand, we can't change the past, no matter how much we may wish differently. The future is what matters. And more importantly, learning as much as we can from one another since the Brevkan are mostly a mystery."

A woman's soft voice said, "Maybe it should stay that way."

The female's skin was a reddish tone, one possessed by the Brevkan but not the Kelderans. She would've had a harder upbringing than he would since Thorin could "pass" as Kelderan. "If you've come only to persuade us to maintain shame and secrecy, then I implore you to leave. I, for one, am here to learn. Any of our futures may depend on it."

The same female replied, "How so?"

"Do you have children?" She shook her head and Thorin glanced at the others. "Do any of you?"

At first, no one moved. However, after a few seconds, a male with golden skin—another Kelderan skin tone that could blend with the rest of the population—raised his hand. "I have a son."

From what little Thorin had been able to discover, male offspring had a harder time dealing with rages and visions than females. Not that either was spared completely. "Is he old enough to have rages?"

The male shook his head. "He's less than a year old."

Which according to Vala's Barren contacts, was when a part Brevkan baby acted like any other. Only after their second birthday did nightmares and other characteristics begin. "And it's for his sake that you're here."

The golden male grunted. "Yes. I don't know much, and while my bride is half-Brevkan as well, together we're clueless and desperate to save our son from the same tortures of our youth."

Thorin resisted a frown. It was the first he'd heard of two half-Brevkan individuals having a child together. "As I may soon be in the same circumstances, I, too, wish to learn as much as possible." Confusion flashed since his bride was one of the Barren, but Thorin continued before anyone could talk. "I will talk more about that with those who truly wish to share. If you agree to meet weekly and talk openly, then we'll all vow the information in this room stays with us and our immediate families. If you don't share the same idea, then please leave now."

The timid female from earlier stood and quickly fled the room.

Maybe he should've asked her name, to keep an eye on her.

Regardless, he knew her face. If she caused trouble and Prince Kason or any of the other members of the leadership brought it to his attention, then he'd act. She shouldn't be followed or questioned for simply wanting to remain hidden and avoid scrutiny.

He focused back on the remaining nine people. "Now that only the committed remain, let's sit more informally and make our vows. And then I suggest sharing any information you've learned over the years."

The golden male asked, "Shouldn't we keep a record?"

Thorin shook his head. "No, we're not taking notes. At least, not for the time being. Written records can easily be leaked, and I want to ensure we learn to trust one another above anything else. I hope sharing information is only the first step."

The golden male smiled. "If you start to say this will turn into our closest circle of friends, I'll have to wonder what happened to the growly general."

He frowned. "Have we met?"

"Not personally. However, I was on one of the same army starships as you. My name is Cellig."

The name Cellig didn't ring a bell. However,

some ships had thousands of crew members, and not even a general as thorough as Thorin could keep track of every individual. "This former general only cares about his bride and making her happy. Any honorable male would do the same."

Cellig nodded. "Agreed."

Understanding passed between the two. Thorin hadn't made many friends or even semi-acquaintances over the years. However, if the male was bold enough to speak and question him, he might be worth getting to know.

As they went around giving names and speaking vows, Thorin's mind kept wandering back to Vala. He trusted Kalahn to look after her, but he was anxious to hold his bride close again and ensure she was safe.

VALA OPENED her eyes and found Kalahn in a chair not far from her bed, furiously scribbling something down onto sheets of paper.

Since she'd seen her friend do the same many times before, Vala knew Kalahn had received important information via telepathy. Whether from a distant planet or someone on Jasvar, she had no idea.

Sitting up, Vala rearranged the blankets and blinked away the lingering drowsiness. With the curtains drawn, she had no idea if it were still daylight or not.

Kalahn's voice filled the room. "You're awake. How're you feeling? Even if all you have is a slight headache, tell me now because I don't want to face Thorin's wrath."

She frowned. "Thorin would never hurt you."

Kalahn waved a hand in dismissal. "Of course not. But if I'm ever to convince him of letting you go to the education retreat in a few months' time, then I need to be on his good side."

"I'd forgotten all about that."

She paused, knowing that if she didn't give an explanation, it would be a red flag to Kalahn. They'd been planning a mini-retreat for the older children of both the Kelderan colony and the Jasvarian one for weeks.

Kalahn's voice softened. "I already know what happened since you mentally projected it during your sleep. However, I'd much rather hear it from you directly."

Vala resisted a sigh. She knew Kalahn was still learning to control her strong telepathic abilities and couldn't always shield out others' thoughts. And yet, the knowledge her friend knew some of her deepest secrets and fears didn't make saying them any easier.

Kalahn moved her chair closer and took Vala's hand. "You can tell me anything, Vala. You know that. I may not be an expert yet in blocking out others, but few can penetrate my mental shields for information."

"What about Ryven?"

Ryven was Kalahn's husband, a former trainer in the Kelderan Army. For anyone who grumbled about how rights and freedom moved too slowly inside the Kelderan colony, they conveniently dismissed how King Keltor and Prince Kason had allowed their sister to marry an orphaned commoner.

Kalahn shrugged. "I can keep him out if I need to. Although hopefully not forever. After all, if what you projected is true, then everyone will find out in time."

Before she could think of why not, the words tumbled from her lips, "Yes, I can apparently have children now. My only grievance is that there is no choice in the matter. My shock at finally being deemed equal under Kelderan law is nothing compared to Thorin's adjustment. It's taken so much coaxing to ease his self-hatred. I couldn't bear it if it flares up again, especially when seeing any child of ours for the first time."

Kalahn squeezed her hand. "Thorin loves you, and pretty much worships you to the point I'm not sure how you deal with it—I'd feel suffocated. Still, he would never blame you. And once he accepts that any child you share would be part you, he'll love it right away."

Vala sighed. "You say that so easily. It's much more complicated than that."

The princess shrugged. "You can believe that if you wish. However, sometimes an outsider can see things you can't. And there's no way Thorin would ever loathe you or anything connected to you. Well, he might grumble a bit as babies are noisy, and often smelly, and take up so much time and brain power."

She smiled at her friend. "So no children in the near future for you then?"

Her friend grimaced. "No way. With my luck, I'd birth a telepathic prodigy and struggle to keep up with them. I'm not saying never, but I want to learn who I truly am with these new powers before trying to help shape any new person."

Kalahn hadn't been born with telepathy. She'd undergone a DNA-splicing procedure, one that had taken well. So much so, she rivaled many natural-born telepathic prodigies. However, her powers were still new, and Vala was one of the few she felt comfortable talking with about her fears of burnout. Or, worse—accidentally killing her lord Ryven by draining his life force for additional power.

Vala replied, "There's no rush. Especially since there's still not a cure for preventing the doom virus from attacking male embryos in the womb." Vala stilled. In all the revelations and confusion, she hadn't really thought about that aspect. Jasvar's male population was critically low, and the virus was the reason.

And even though she'd been afraid of becoming pregnant and losing Thorin, she was starting to realize it would happen. In that case, losing her child would be unbearable.

Whether from reading her expression or her thoughts, Vala had no clue, but Kalahn patted her hand and said, "Don't worry. The Kelderan scientists are making progress on that virus. Besides, given how stubborn both you and Thorin are, there's no way a child of yours would succumb to something as lowly as a virus."

She snorted. "If only that were true." Wanting to change the subject for a bit and better control her emotions, Vala motioned toward the sheets of paper in Kalahn's lap. "Can you tell me the latest news?"

"It's nothing too sensitive, really. My brother Keltor had a few policy matters for Kason. He also wanted to share that he discovered the gender of his latest child and insists on giving it a name beginning with the letter K."

At the disdain in Kalahn's voice, Vala couldn't help but laugh. "It's tradition, as you well know, for the Kelderan royal family to do that. And since your brother is king now, it seems fitting."

Kalahn rolled her eyes. "But you'd think Keltor would want to modernize a little in that regard. I lose track of all the names and I'm a member of the royal family. I can't imagine anyone else keeping them straight."

"I could list them all easily," Vala stated.

Kalahn stuck out her tongue. "Well, not all of us have such good memories."

She chuckled, and nearly pulled Kalahn into a hug. However, a lifetime spent avoiding contact with anyone who wasn't one of the Barren was hard to crack, even when it came to her best friend.

Vala leaned forward a fraction. "Well, are you going to share the name? I won't tell anyone, I promise."

Kalahn sighed. "They're having a girl and will name her Kerralyn. I'll admit Kerra is pretty, but still, if I ever have a baby, they won't have a name beginning with K. Ever. Not even as one of the letters."

Laughing, Vala chatted with Kalahn about some of the other tidbits of news she'd received. The distraction, combined with her friend's lively personality, helped Vala forget some of her fears for the moment.

And who knew, maybe Thorin would have more good news from his meeting. She had no choice but to be hopeful.

THORIN ENTERED his apartment to find Vala laughing. Given how Kalahn was gesticulating wildly, it probably had something to do with the princess.

However, he barely paid attention to the other female. Merely seeing his bride enjoying herself sent a surge of love through his body. Without thinking, he closed the distance to her, cupped her face, and kissed her thoroughly.

Vala's surprise quickly faded and she met his tongue stroke for stroke, both of them trying to outdo the other.

It was only when Kalahn cleared her throat extremely loudly that Thorin stopped. With a growl, he looked at the princess and said, "You can leave now."

Vala touched his arm. "Thorin, be nice. Kalahn's my friend, and you promised."

Kalahn put up her hands. "Don't worry, I should be going anyway. My own lord will be searching for me soon if I don't meet him for our dinner date." Kalahn paused and added as she stared at Vala, "Call me anytime, Vala. Okay?"

"I will. Thanks, Kalahn."

The princess stood straight and bobbed her head curtly at Thorin. "General."

He sighed. "Stop being silly and go to your lord."

"Right, because you told me to so I must," Kalahn drawled. However, before he could say anything else to convince the female to leave, Kalahn dashed to the door, her long skirts flowing behind her. Her expression turned serious. "Don't hurt her, Thorin. Otherwise, you'll have to deal with me."

Thorin knew little about telepathy, but he was wise enough to understand a strong one could damage another person's mind, maybe even permanently. While he'd like to think Kalahn wasn't one to seek vengeance, he couldn't be sure.

Vala said, "He won't. Goodbye, Kalahn."

After another few seconds of glaring, Kalahn left.

Thorin sat beside his bride on the couch. She instantly leaned against him and he wrapped his arms around her. They sat that way for a few seconds, her scent and heat soothing him as they always did.

Vala eventually broke the silence. "How did your meeting go?"

Since his vow to the others at the meeting allowed him to share their secrets with his bride, he didn't hold back. "Nine others ended up staying and committed themselves to meet weekly for the foreseeable future."

She raised her head. "That's wonderful, and far more than we expected."

"True." He hesitated, not wanting to ruin the current atmosphere of talk about the future. However, he owed Vala the truth. "One of them even has a son. Not quite a year old, but still, he shared a lot about his experience so far."

His bride laid a hand on his jaw and gently turned his head until he met her gaze. "And how do you feel after talking with him about it?"

He grunted. "It's harder to hate an existing child than an abstract concept."

Vala tilted her head, in the way she usually did before she asked for something. "Do you think the male could bring his family over for dinner one night?"

Thorin blinked. That was one of the last things he'd expected for her to want. "What? Why?"

"While I appreciate any knowledge you can share, I'd like to hear about it all for myself. Besides, I have questions you may not think of. Especially for the mother."

He shook his head. "Both of the parents are half-Brevkan, so it's not quite the same."

Vala smiled. "Maybe not. But if I end up carrying your baby one day, then I want to find out everything I can."

He searched her gaze. "Because you're afraid?"

"Maybe a little, but mostly so I can be prepared and ensure the best future for us. Since I'm not part Brevkan, maybe there's something I should know. Especially since I would never be able to ask your mother."

Even if his mother's mind wasn't fading, talking about her pregnancy would be cruel. His mother hadn't had an easy time of it, being raped by an enemy and then deciding to keep the resulting child.

Vala's voice filled the room again. "Besides, if they come here, that means I don't have to go out. I thought you'd like that."

Thorin knew his bride would keep trying to lay it on thick, so he said, "I'll see what I can do, although I can't make any promises."

She moved to sit in his lap, and he wrapped his arms around her. Her radiant smile sent a course of heat throughout his entire body.

Not that he'd claim her anytime soon. His bride needed to rest.

But he'd never tire of her. Never

"Kiss me, Thorin, and then we'll plan the dinner for your new friend."

If not distracted by the delectable female in his lap, Thorin would say Cellig wasn't his friend yet. However, as Vala pressed her lips to his, he forgot about everything else but the delicious heat and taste of his bride.

Chapter Five

Vala had done her best to ease Thorin's anxiety in the days leading up to the dinner with Cellig and his family. And yet, she watched as Thorin adjusted one thing and then another, muttering, "This isn't safe for a child. Or this. Maybe I should cancel."

He never waited for Vala to say it was too late to cancel, or remind him of how he'd vowed to attend the dinner no matter what. And in a way, his nervousness and thoughtfulness only made her heart warm.

For a male who'd feared children for so long, he cared deeper than he probably realized.

And it was the first time Vala truly thought they would be okay. There would still be problems and trials in their future, but if children honestly repulsed or scared him, he wouldn't worry so much about one he'd never met before.

The door chimed and Thorin waltzed over to it before Vala could do more than blink. He opened the door, revealing a male with golden skin and a female next to him with purple skin, a child on her hip. The interesting thing was how the child also had purple skin. It wasn't a Brevkan skin tone. Even with both of his parents having some of that heritage, the boy had ended up with a Kelderan color.

Thorin motioned them inside. Once he shut the door, he gestured toward her. "This is my bride, Vala."

Since it was usually custom for the male to do the introductions, Vala resisted blinking when the female spoke up. "I'm Pallyn. This is my lord, Cellig, and our son, Myden."

The baby patted his hand against his mother's breast, almost as if claiming she was his.

Her entire life, Vala had viewed children with mixed feelings. On the one hand, they were mostly treasured in Kelderan culture and given priority. And on the other, not being able to have one had sentenced Vala to a life of exile she hadn't chosen.

However, things had changed completely. She was no longer an outcast and could even have one of her own someday. Of course, that brought on a new set of problems.

None of which should be projected onto the

innocent child, though. Moving next to Pallyn, Vala
tickled the baby's neck. He squealed and hid his head
against his mother's side.

Such a common reaction, and yet in that
moment, Vala desperately wanted a child of her own
to hold, cuddle, and love no matter what their
genetics contained.

Pallyn lightly jostled her son until he sat up again.
She said, "No need to be shy, Myden. You love tickles
and Miss Vala here looks as if she wants to do it
again."

Vala shared a glance with the woman, and they
smiled at one another. Pallyn may not be a Barren,
but she'd endured her own set of challenges due to
her Brevkan heritage.

Meaning they had more in common than she'd
originally realized.

Myden reached out a chubby purple hand and
Vala took it. As the little boy wrapped his fingers
around one of hers, Cellig's voice filled the room.
"Come, Thorin. Let's get everyone drinks while the
females entertain the little one."

Drink-serving was another thing Kelderan
females usually handled, so Vala's gaze moved to
Cellig. Pallyn whispered, "Yes, Cellig is different in
many ways, and not just because of who his father
was. It's why I married him. How about we sit down?
Myden looks small, but he weighs more than you
think."

It was on the tip of Vala's tongue to offer to take him, but she resisted. After all, she was virtually a stranger still.

Slowly removing her finger, Vala guided Pallyn and Myden to the sofa. Once they sat down, Pallyn made silly faces at her son as she said, "I had hoped moving to Jasvar would better our lives, but what your lord has done so far exceeded our expectations. To show our gratitude, feel free to ask anything. Cellig explained your situation, and it must be disorienting for you. Let us help."

Vala stared at the woman playing with her baby. She finally made her mouth work. "Thank you. You merely accepting the invitation for tonight means a lot to me."

Pallyn met her gaze. "We've both been formal and polite, so that's done and over with. I'd rather be straightforward and save us both a lot of trouble."

Even if Pallyn wasn't part Brevkan, she never would've fit into the patriarchal ideal back on Keldera. "You remind me of a few people I know."

"Then you should introduce me, if it's possible. Cellig and I have mostly kept to ourselves over the years, for reasons you can guess. But I'm not introverted and would love to get out more."

She watched the baby trying to stand and jump with his mother's help. Vala asked, "What about your son? Do you have someone to watch him?"

"Myden is pretty easygoing, as far as babies are

concerned. However, Cellig loves watching him, too, when he can. So it shouldn't be a problem."

Cellig's voice jumped in. "It's true. I've never understood why a male is supposed to scoff at spending time with his children. At one time, I never thought I'd ever find a bride, let alone have a child. So I treasure both with everything I have."

The couple shared a loving glance, and Vala couldn't help but seek out Thorin's gaze. His expression was unreadable, which meant he was conflicted. She burned to ask if Cellig had said something to him in the kitchen but didn't want to do it in front of the pair. So Vala stood and went to her husband's side, to lean against him. As soon as his arm wrapped around her waist, the tension of his muscles eased.

Cellig passed his bride a drink and picked up his son. After swinging him gently, he held him close and walked over to Thorin. "You asked why I wanted to be your second-in-command in finding and connecting those with Brevkan ancestry, and Myden is the reason. He deserves much better than we did growing up. I hope you'll consider my request seriously."

Thorin grunted at the same time Myden leaned over and touched Thorin's arm. Then the baby leaned over more, extending both of his arms.

Cellig chuckled. "He likes you. Will you hold him?"

Vala's initial reaction was to make excuses so her lord wouldn't have to be rude.

However, as Thorin stared at the baby, her gut told her to hold her tongue.

And so she waited to see what her husband would do.

THORIN STARED at the tiny male, his arms outstretched, and struggled with what to do.

He'd never held such a young child in his life, and he didn't want to hurt him. Especially if he took up Cellig's offer to share the enormity of the task ahead, concerning those with Brevkan ancestry.

But then he remembered the happiness on his bride's face when she'd played with the boy earlier. If Thorin truly wanted to prove he would love any child she gave him, this would be a perfect opportunity to show how he didn't hate children.

Releasing his bride at his side, Thorin gently picked up the baby boy and held Myden up in front of him. The little boy kicked his legs and almost succeeded in hitting Thorin's chin.

Cellig spoke up. "You can gently toss him. He loves it."

The thought of tossing anything so tiny and helpless sent a rush of horror throughout his body. "I don't want to hurt him."

Vala's soft, soothing voice whispered into his ear, "You never would, zylar. Just hold him against your body. It'll be easier."

Baby Myden tilted his head and blinked. It was almost as if he were encouraging Thorin.

Which was preposterous. He was a baby.

Slowly, Thorin maneuvered Myden to his side. The child stopped kicking and instead lightly dug his nails into Thorin's skin.

Celling said, "Be gentle, Myden. You don't want to draw blood against a former general."

The words were said in a teasing tone, and Thorin relaxed. "Maybe I'll have to teach him self-defense, then, once he can walk."

The corner of Cellig's mouth ticked up. "Maybe a few years after that. Otherwise, Myden might start an underground toddler fight club. I'm sure that would land us all in trouble with the colony's council."

Vala sighed. "You're planning lessons for a baby and yet, I couldn't get self-defense lessons until this past year simply because I'm female." She touched his arm and Thorin met his bride's gaze. "Will you be all right if I sit with Pallyn?"

His female tried to hide it, but he saw the concern in her eyes. Even without saying a word, he knew it was for him and not out of fear he'd hurt the child.

He'd never get used to such utter and complete

trust.

Little Myden dug his nails even deeper, but Thorin didn't flinch. He looked the little boy in the eye and said calmly yet firmly, "No nails."

The boy stared and relaxed his grip.

Cellig chuckled. "Maybe your talents were wasted in the army. You clearly have a knack for baby whispering."

Thorin grunted in approval at the baby. "Good job, Myden." The little boy tried to bounce in place and Thorin adjusted his hold to accommodate it. He met Cellig's gaze again. "They are little people. I don't know how to treat them any differently."

Vala touched his arm. "Your way seems to work with Myden." Amusement danced in her eyes. "Who knows, maybe if it works on others, you can open a baby whispering class."

He reached out and lightly slapped his female's rear. "Go sit with Pallyn. I have a few things to discuss with Cellig."

After she kissed him on the cheek and tickled Myden one last time—the joy on her face was one he would never tire of—Thorin focused all his energy on Cellig. He'd put off answering the male's request long enough. "I understand your offer to help me with my task is sincere, but it will be time-consuming. That means being apart from your bride and son more than you may like."

Cellig shrugged. "They'll help, too, when they

can. After all, Pallyn isn't the sort to sit and watch as things happen."

"My bride isn't either," he muttered.

Cellig grinned. "Good, then you won't fight me on treating a female as an equal, especially regarding intelligence. If anything, Pallyn is smarter than me."

"I assume nothing about anyone until I meet and evaluate them. It's how I functioned in the army, and how I plan to live my life."

Myden squirmed and reached for his father. Thorin quickly handed the little boy over and watched as he curled against Cellig's side and sucked his thumb.

Cellig brushed the faint wisps of silver hair from the boy's face. "He'll fall asleep soon. But don't worry, once he does, my son sleeps through most anything. Let me coax him to drift off and then we can have dinner without any interruptions or distractions."

As he watched Cellig walk to the far corner of the room and gently rock his baby, Thorin imagined himself doing the same with a little boy or girl, one with Vala's golden skin and white hair.

He expected a scene of his child much older and screaming in pain from a horrific rage vision to flash. However, it didn't come.

Thorin wasn't one to pin false hopes, but maybe there was something to be done. Living in the open about his heritage would give the added benefit of additional research. No doubt Iljan's analysis of Thorin's samples would only be the beginning.

Not to mention Jasvar held all sorts of flora and fauna that might help tame the pain and instability.

True, maybe nothing would ever help. But Vala's love had soothed him, and maybe the combination of his and Vala's love for their child would be enough to prevent the worst.

Nothing was guaranteed, but Thorin was already fond of little Myden. He imagined it'd be even more intense with his own offspring, especially after watching Vala grow round with their child.

He searched out Vala and watched as she spoke animatedly about something with the other female. Her love had done so much to heal him already. Proof of their love might take it even further. After all, Thorin would never hurt a child. And that meant never succumbing to a rage vision.

Once the dinner was over, he'd tell Vala. And then he'd claim his female without regret, knowing full well what could happen. It was time to change his life's path once more. He may be a little nervous, but not reluctant. Vala was worth anything to him. And he'd spend the rest of his life proving it to her.

Chapter Six

No sooner had Vala said her goodbyes to Cellig, Pallyn, and Myden and shut the door before Thorin came up behind her and wrapped his arms around her body. Nuzzling her neck, he murmured, "I love you, zyla. Will you let me claim you tonight?"

She did her best not to tense. His words held a much deeper meaning than usual.

Thorin was willing to father a child.

Raising a hand behind her to his jaw, she turned his face so she could look into his eyes. She didn't want to doubt him, but the end result from his claiming could be monumental. "While I'm more than ready for you, zylar, are you sure?"

One of his hands moved upward, to cup her breast. "Yes, more than anything. My thoughts kept straying tonight. Not to any sort of nightmare but rather of me holding a tiny baby that looked just like you, and it didn't frighten me. Nervous, a little, but not afraid." He gently squeezed her breast. "You've shown me how love can transform and help a person. I want to believe we can do the same for our child."

Emotion choked her throat. She didn't realize how much she'd been trying to hold off her want, her desire, of finally being able to have a child of her own with the man she loved. Something she'd never thought possible.

But it looked like it may happen after all. And without any resentment or hatred.

Forcing herself to swallow and clear her throat, she finally whispered, "I love you, Thorin."

"I hope so, because I'm not going anywhere."

She smiled and turned in his arms to face him. "Good, because I'm honestly considering the baby whispering idea."

His lips twitched. "Maybe for Kason's daughter, once she's born. And only so I can annoy him."

Vala laughed. Thorin wasn't as easygoing or teasing as other males, but he wasn't afraid to show his humor with her every once in a while. "I'm sure Taryn would love that. She's always looking for ways to irritate her lord and tease him to no end."

Taryn Demara was not only Kason's bride but the human colony's leader. It was still funny to think that if Taryn hadn't tricked Kason's spaceship into believing they were helpless females and then kidnapping him, Vala and Thorin wouldn't be standing together in each other's arms.

Never had she been so grateful for someone else's actions.

He placed his forehead against hers, his eyes turning heated. "I'll keep that in mind. But for now, I only want to think of you."

With a growl, he took her lips in a demanding kiss. She opened her mouth, inviting him, and with each stroke, lick, and nibble, her legs grew weaker and heat spread throughout her body.

Before she knew it, he scooped her up and carried her to their bed. After laying her down, he crawled on his hands and knees over her, caging her body. A thrill went through her at the large, muscled male above her. She whispered, "Don't hold back with me, Thorin. I want all of you out in the open, more than ever before."

His eyes began to glow as he sat back on his heels and freed his straining cock. The sight of his long, hard erection poking from the opening in his trousers made her squirm.

Leaning down, Thorin kissed her, his lips and tongue claiming her in forceful, determined motions. With each of her whimpers, he increased his intensity, to the point she could barely breathe.

He finally broke the kiss right before she was afraid she'd pass out. His eyes glowed a brighter blue than she'd ever seen before. His husky voice rolled over her. "I hope you're ready for me, love. Let's see."

His large, warm hand ran down the front of her body, lightly tweaked her sensitive nipples, and then continued the journey downward. Every slow inch was torture, in a good way, making her hotter and almost desperate to have him inside her.

As soon as he reached the hem of her dress, he tossed it up to her waist and spread her legs wide. For a second, he merely sat there staring at her exposed center, each second making her more swollen and wet. "Thorin, please. Claim me."

He lightly ran a finger through her center, and she bucked her hips upward at the touch. She'd always be attuned to her lord's touch, but something was different tonight. For a split second, she wondered if it had to do with his Brevkan half, priming her for his seed.

But then Thorin placed his cock at her entrance and she forgot about everything but the way he stretched her inch by inch.

Once he was finally to the hilt, Vala was on the verge of panting.

It was almost as if his cock was warming up inside her and growing even thicker.

Maybe it would scare some, but Vala loved it and craved more.

She reached out and dug her nails into his arms. "No holding back, remember?"

Thorin's eyes went from glowing to a near blaze. Pinning her arms over her head, he lowered his lips until they were a few inches from hers and then moved his hips. He was thicker, warmer, and somehow managed to stroke every secret spot inside her with his movements.

Digging in her nails deeper, she moaned out, "Faster."

With a growl, Thorin complied, increasing the force of his thrusts, their bed moving in a dangerous fashion.

Not that Vala cared. Damn, her entire body was strung tight, on the verge of orgasm despite the fact he wasn't playing with her nipples, which was how Kelderan females came.

Then he growled, thrust one last time, and her world exploded, her vision filling with pure brightness and temporarily blinding her as wave after wave of pleasure swept through her every cell. It was so close to pain, but oh so good.

As Thorin's glowing body dimmed, her vision started to return. Despite her sudden exhaustion, she put it together. "I couldn't see because of you."

He stroked the hair off her damp forehead. "I can't explain it, but it was somehow like my entire life and purpose depended on this moment. Then the room went as bright as a star."

She lifted a hand to his cheek and lightly played

with his jaw. "I know you hate it when I say it, but you're so beautiful when you glow, Thorin."

He grunted, but not before she saw a small smile. As if to distract her, he kissed her. Thorin took his time exploring her mouth as if it were the first time. When he finally pulled away, she asked, "Maybe we can try that again?"

"My insatiable bride." He kissed her gently. "I would love nothing more, but there's a problem."

Vala raised an eyebrow. "Are you getting older and need some time to rest?"

He narrowed his eyes. "I'm not old."

She laughed. "Of course not. But unless you tell me the reason, then I'll have to go with you not having the same stamina as a few weeks ago."

One of his hands strayed to her breast and lightly tweaked her nipple through the fabric. "I'm debating whether to tell you the truth, as it's nearly as bad."

Her need to tease vanished. "What's wrong?"

He kissed the corner of her mouth. "Don't worry, zyla. It's not that bad. I'm just, er, stuck."

"Stuck?"

"As in, my cock swelled and I can't pull out."

"So I was right! I thought you'd grown in size."

He drawled, "While I'm glad you're not horrified, it could be a problem if it doesn't shrink a little."

She grinned. "You have an erection-deflating list, remember? What was the first one again? Oh, that's right—thinking about the death birds on Jasvar, the ones that can pick your bones clean in a matter of minutes."

He sighed. "We may have made a child tonight and that's what you want me to think about on this occasion?"

The need to tease had fully returned. "Well, it'll make an interesting story."

"We're not telling anyone about this, except for maybe the doctor."

She took his face between her hands. "It's probably another thing related to the Brevkan. Maybe you can ask some of the others about it."

Thorin turned his head to nip her fingers. "Right now, I only want to think of you, zyla. I didn't take care of you first, as I always do. I'm sorry."

"Don't apologize. I've never orgasmed so hard in my life. You're quite the lover, Thorin Jarrell. I may have to share that information with some of my female friends."

"I don't want to know what you females talk about," he muttered.

She giggled. "No, I don't think you do."

His gaze zeroed in on hers again. "Now I'm curious."

"Try to top this time, and maybe I'll share."

Thorin tentatively moved his hips, and she felt him leave her body.

Before she could say a word, Thorin was up and disappeared into the bathroom. He quickly reappeared naked, carrying a wet cloth. He remained silent as he sat down and cleaned between her thighs.

Since a Kelderan male usually only did something similar after claiming a virgin bride for the first time, it made her eyes water a little. She couldn't imagine a more thoughtful and caring male if she tried.

Once he finished, he tossed the cloth away and positioned himself between her thighs. "Unless you've changed your mind, I'm out to prove I can top even myself."

"You're not going to suddenly have a second penis spring out and keep me pinned in place with their combined girth, are you?"

Humor danced in his eyes. "I have no idea, love. Let's find out."

And while Thorin solidly had only one penis for the rest of the evening, he did make her scream and moan louder each time he claimed her, and Vala had no complaints.

Chapter Seven

Thorin tried his best to make his face a little less scary, as Cellig kept putting it. Since smiling always made the blasted male laugh, Thorin avoided that and went with something he'd learned from Vala —what she called the "Barren expression of placid existence."

Of course, placid wasn't a word most people used to describe Thorin. However, it'd been the best option so far, one that didn't make Cellig lose his breath from laughter.

Cellig finally nodded. "Maybe the female will at least open the door now."

He grunted. "Then let's get on with it. This is the last person we're visiting today and I'm anxious to get home."

Not that he would bring up his reason to Cellig,

even if Cellig's bride probably knew why Thorin was eager to go home.

Today he and Vala would find out if they'd successfully conceived or not.

Cellig motioned forward with one hand. They walked down the last bit of the hallway, toward the apartment that should contain Yelka, an older female who was half-Brevkan. If their information was correct, then she would've been born during the early days of the Brevkan war back on Keldera.

The fact she'd made it to nearly fifty and wasn't insane was a good sign. On top of that, only healthy adults had been granted permission to join the Kelderan colony on Jasvar, meaning the female hadn't suffered any strange ailments in all those years, either. Or at least none that had resulted in permanent injury.

They stopped in front of the correct door. Since Cellig was the more affable out of them, he always handled the majority of the talking when they met other part Brevkan individuals for the first time. That suited Thorin just fine since it meant he could watch them closely for ticks or signs of fear, nervousness, or even deceit.

While he was starting to believe a mixed parentage often produced stable, somewhat normal individuals, Thorin would always have a healthy dose of skepticism. It was how he'd survived so long with his secret, and he needed to keep it up to protect his family going forward.

Cellig glanced at Thorin's face one last time before knocking. The door soon opened to reveal a female with light blue skin and black hair mixed with a few strands of white. She glanced between them. "I wondered when you'd get round to visiting me."

Cellig didn't bat an eye. "Everyone said you kept an ear to the ground, and I see they were right."

The female who had to be Yelka shrugged. "Haven't we all? Otherwise, none of us would be standing here right now."

Thorin rather liked the female's directness. Sensing she wouldn't balk at his approach, Thorin jumped in. "Then let's not waste time. Ask any questions you wish, although it may be more prudent to do it either inside your apartment or inside one of the shared meeting spaces we've reserved, to avoid any accidental eavesdroppers."

Yelka studied him a second before replying, "I'll come, but only if my daughter comes with me, too."

Interesting. No one they'd talked to had mentioned Yelka having a daughter. However, seeing yet another generation with possibly diluted Brevkan heritage—if she were Yelka's biological child—would be the most relevant to Thorin and his bride.

Cellig nodded. "Of course she can accompany you. We'll wait here while you fetch her."

Yelka disappeared into her apartment and

reappeared shortly with another female in her twenties. She had the magenta skin tone Kelderans had, but not Brevkans—Brevkans were usually yellow, blue, or a deeper shade of red.

Yelka waved toward her daughter. "This is my daughter, Orlain. I see questions burning in your eyes but hold your tongue until we're inside the meeting room. Which one is it?"

Cellig gave the location and the older female walked right past them without another word. Thorin almost snorted at her antics, but kept his reaction in check.

He suspected the human female leader, Taryn, would approve of Yelka's ways.

Only once the daughter followed her mother did he and Cellig bring up the rear. And despite Cellig's sometimes annoying faults of teasing and joking, the male knew when to keep quiet. It was one of the reasons Thorin kept working with the male to uncover the hidden Brevkans inside the Kelderan colony.

Since the meeting room was on the same level as Yelka's apartment, they reached it quickly and all settled inside. Once they all sat around a table, Yelka raised her brows. "Well? What questions do you have?"

Yelka's daughter sighed but didn't say anything.

Thorin motioned for Cellig to start and the male cleared his throat. "I'm sure you've heard the rumors about how we're locating and trying to talk with each and every part Brevkan individual inside the Kelderan colony. As was hinted by some of the Barren who cared for many of us as children, there are quite a few of us here on Jasvar. They pulled strings and called in favors to give so many of us the chance of a better life. In return, Thorin and I are trying to connect all of us so that we can learn from one another, as well as support each other, if needed."

Yelka huffed. "Yes, yes, I've heard that already. But while it sounds grand, it also sounds risky. One negative report or misdeed and we could all be sent back to Keldera. And while things are different here inside the colony, that's not the case back on Keldera. Unless you have some sort of proof we are safe, then I have no wish to talk with you."

Maybe some people would beg, or perhaps use fancy words to try to sway Yelka to their side. However, Thorin didn't operate that way. Retrieving a specially preserved laminated document from the bag he carried, he placed it on the table. "This is a signed guarantee by both the human leader of Jasvar and the king of Keldera that no one will be removed from this planet as long as they wish to remain. Of course, it doesn't mean we can commit crimes and go unpunished. But any such event will be tried and sentenced here as well."

Yelka pulled the precious sheet closer to her and

read it slowly. It was her daughter who finally spoke again. "This is beyond anything you could've expected, Mother. I think they're sincere."

The older female huffed. "Maybe I've coddled you too much over the years, Orlain. Politicians and royalty notoriously break their promises, as has happened many times in the past."

Thorin spoke before Cellig could. "I understand your skepticism—we all have it to some degree. However, living in secluded fear has only made it that much harder for us over the years. If we don't try to change things, they'll remain the same forever. And I don't know about you, but I don't want that status quo for any child of mine. Don't you want to make a better future for your daughter?"

The older woman clicked her tongue. "That's right, you've married the Barren who can now conceive. And if you're curious, the change is permanent. The same thing happened to me."

Thorin frowned and glanced to her forehead, which didn't have the legally required tattoo for all Barren females on Keldera.

Yelka continued, "And no, I wasn't with the Barren. My mother raised me in secret, in a remote part of the world, and I found out the change happened in my early twenties quite by accident."

Thorin opened his mouth, but Yelka's daughter spoke first. "What my mother isn't telling you is that she was kidnapped by a group of Brevkan warriors toward the very end of the war."

Even without Orlain finishing the story, Thorin knew what had come next—rape. Probably repeatedly.

And Yelka had barely been an adult at the time.

Under the table, he clenched his fingers into a fist. He may be part Brevkan, but he would never stop hating the bastards for ruining so many lives during the war.

And if it came to another battle with them, Thorin wouldn't hesitate to sign up and fight.

Yelka finally spoke up. "I can see the burning hatred in your eyes, but they aren't worth your time, lad. A Kelderan squad killed them, about three months after I was taken. The Kelderans were kind and took me to a base camp to recover since the closest hospital was too far away. I kept planning my escape, hoping to achieve it before they discovered I couldn't have children. But then as pregnancy symptoms set in, and a doctor confirmed it, my true identity was kept a secret from there on out."

Thorin didn't want to upset the female, but there was something he had to ask. "Was there a red band around your leg at first?"

"Yes," Yelka stated. "And it faded over time."

Which all but confirmed that what had happened to Vala was the same.

Thorin jumped in before Cellig could say

anything. "I know you're skeptical about what we do. And even if you don't wish to come forth or talk with a group, will you at least talk with my bride? She had the same red band and went through the same changes. She's always curious and would probably find a way to communicate with you anyway."

Yelka snorted. "But this way you can keep track of her?" He grunted, but he couldn't say anything before she spoke again. "I have no trouble talking with your bride, especially given everything she's been trying to do for the Barren and the females in general inside the colony. All I ask is for you not to pressure me about joining your movement. Maybe with time I'll feel comfortable, but I'm not there yet."

Her daughter said softly, "What about me? Are there any others who are three-quarters Brevkan, like I am?"

So, Orlain was Yelka's biological daughter, with a Brevkan father. Thorin had assumed as much, but now he knew for certain.

He shared a glance with Cellig and nodded. The other male responded calmly, "We haven't found any other three-quarters Brevkan children yet. However, there are some close to your age who are half Brevkan, if that will help?"

Orlain bobbed her head. "I'd like that. Then we can both find out what we have in common, or what's different."

As the female kept her gaze downward and drew

circles on the table, Thorin wondered if it was a coping mechanism to tame her rage visions or if she was merely afraid to be anything else, in case her Brevkan heritage showed its true colors.

He had no bloody idea how a three-quarters individual would act.

Not that he would assume anything bad about Orlain without supporting facts. No doubt the female had already had a tough life, and maybe she needed friendship and acceptance to blossom into her true self.

He resisted a frown at that thought. Yes, Vala had definitely rubbed off on him.

Cellig handed a small card to Orlain. "This has both of our addresses inside the colony, as well as information about the meetings. Feel free to visit us anytime."

Orlain took the card. "Thank you. When's the next meeting?"

Yelka harrumphed. "Are you sure you want to do this, sweet? Once you out yourself, there's no turning back. And once word spreads about how you're more Brevkan than Kelderan, it may not end well for you."

The younger female turned her body toward her mother. "I love you, Mother, but I can't keep hiding away. I want to live life before I'm too old to do so."

While he didn't know much about the fancy of females, he suspected Orlain wanted the chance to have fun and maybe even fall in love.

Of course, he couldn't push away the small voice inside his head that sounded a lot like Vala, saying maybe there was something more she wanted to do with her life than get married.

Thank goodness they could remain on Jasvar indefinitely. Neither he nor Vala would do well if forced back into the constrained rules of society on Keldera.

Since the two females continued to smile at each other, he cleared his throat. "Unless there is anything else you wish to know, we should go. My bride is waiting for me."

Yelka met his gaze once more. "Tell her that I'll stop by to visit tomorrow."

He blinked. "Tomorrow?"

The older woman replied, "Yes, tomorrow. I don't like putting things off. I'll come by in the morning, so let her know."

Yelka hadn't asked but instructed. He resisted a frown. "I will ask her first."

She waved a hand. "She has no classes or lessons then, so she'll say yes."

"How do you—"

Yelka cut him off. "I know just about everything that happens inside the colony. And if I'm right, you're anxious to get back to your bride for some news."

He wanted to demand how she knew that, but resisted. Thorin felt Cellig's eyes on him—he was one of the few who knew he and Vala would find out the pregnancy test results today, thanks to Vala becoming fast friends with his bride—but ignored the other male. "Maybe you should consider working for the colony's security branch. They could use someone as resourceful as you."

Yelka grinned. "I just might. But for now, shoo. Don't keep your bride waiting. And remember, I'll see her in the morning, although not too early. I'll give you some privacy."

In nearly three decades, Thorin couldn't remember a time he'd had to fight a blush. But right then and there, he wasn't sure if his cheeks had darkened or not. For crying out loud, the female was insinuating that he and Vala would be having sex all night and into the morning.

Cellig laughed. "I hope you do keep in touch, Yelka. Anyone who can unsettle Thorin is someone I admire."

He punched Cellig's bicep before standing. "We'll be going now." He moved his gaze to the daughter. "I hope to see you at the next meeting, Orlain."

"I'll be there," she answered.

Thorin waited for Cellig to also stand and they made their exit.

As Cellig jibed him the whole way down one corridor and then the next, until they parted ways, Thorin barely paid him any attention. The older female was right—he was anxious to see Vala.

Because it was possible that his life would change forever in the next half hour.

And he wanted to get the next chapter started sooner rather than later.

VALA TRIED to focus on the new Jasvarian recipe she'd received from one of the human colonists, but she'd read the first line at least ten times and still hadn't processed it. Instead, she glanced at the clock again. Thorin should've been home already. And with each minute that passed, she grew more anxious.

Mostly because she wasn't entirely sure how he'd react to her news.

Looking back at the sheet of purple-tinted paper, Vala tried to read the recipe. However, a second later, she heard the door open and close.

Vala rushed from the kitchen and straight to Thorin, who was already striding toward her. She hugged him, and his arms engulfed her instantly. The feel of his warm, hard body against hers always soothed her.

He murmured, "Tell me, zyla."

Taking a deep breath, she forced her head up to look into his gaze. "I'm pregnant."

He blinked a second before his lips curled upward slowly. "From the way you were acting, I'd feared the opposite."

"Feared?"

He stroked her cheek. "I'll admit I was terrified at first, when I learned of the changes. However, the more I work with the others who have part Brevkan children, the more I see them being loved and living mostly normal lives. And to have one with you, the light of my heart? I can't imagine a better gift."

Normally she'd tease him about going soft and romantic, but her eyes prickled with tears and she did her best not to cry. "Thorin, I, well, it's strange. I'd been reconciled to a certain life for so long, and when a new possibility dangled in front of me, I was afraid it was a dream I'd never had. I still want to help orphaned children, and maybe even adopt one, but this baby is more than merely ours. It's a symbol of how much is possible in this life. And now, I think we can do just about anything as long as we're together."

Instead of speaking, Thorin took her lips in a slow, lingering kiss. The familiar taste of her lord washed away her impending tears, replacing it with anticipation and relief.

Thorin wanted both her and their child, and not merely out of some sense of duty, either.

When he finally pulled away, he murmured, "I'm usually more pessimistic, but the longer I'm with you, the harder it is for me to think everything will turn to hell in the end."

She smiled. "That almost sounds like optimism, which is quite a feat for you."

He growled. "You've just told me the best news since you agreed to be my bride, and you decide to tease me now?"

Laughing, Vala hugged him tighter. "If we're going to work on your humor before the baby's born, I'd best start now."

At the mention of a baby, Thorin slid a hand down until he covered her lower abdomen. "Our child."

Her eyes prickled again as she placed her hand over his and lightly squeezed. It was a simple gesture, but never had she loved her lord more. "Yes, and he or she will be so loved. Not to mention if they do suffer from any visions or rages, we'll always work on ways to ease them or stop them entirely. I don't know if you're aware, but I can be stubborn. Much like my lord."

He snorted. "This colony is full of stubborn people. I imagine we'll have a whole generation of rebels, just to spite us."

"Then so be it. Because at least they'll have more freedom and the choice to be with whomever they wish."

Thorin laid his forehead against hers, his hot breath dancing across her lips as he said, "I love you, Vala Yarlen."

She gently guided his hand from her belly to her

breast. "Then maybe you should remind me of how much."

Without a word, Thorin kissed her and spent the next few hours doing exactly that, until they fell into an exhausted slumber.

Epilogue

Roughly Eight Months Later

Thorin stared down at the tiny bundle in his arms, resisting the urge to pull his daughter close and take a deep inhale of her skin again.

Vala teased him about baby-sniffing, and he didn't mind it with her. However, he, Vala, and their daughter were no longer alone. A group far larger than he would've liked filled their apartment, everyone waiting for a turn with his little Hayla.

As he traced the delicate features of Hayla's golden skin, Prince Kason tro el Vallen walked up to him and murmured, "You know our brides are already planning for them to be best friends."

Kason and his bride, Taryn, had had a daughter

as well, several months earlier. Thorin grunted softly, so as to not wake Hayla. "I don't know if that's a good idea. Your daughter is bound to be a bad influence."

Kason raised his dark blue brows. "Mine will be the bad influence? If what our brides have planned comes to fruition, I suspect they will work together to corrupt all others their age. Even my sister Kajala's son, who's nearly a year older, will probably fall under their combined spell."

The prince could've easily brought up the fact that Hayla was part Brevkan, and maybe she would slip up during her training and have a raging outburst. They were rare but tended to happen a few times at two or three years old, no matter what anyone had tried so far. It was one of the many things he and Cellig had discovered during their work.

Not that Thorin was going to sit passively and let it happen. He, Cellig, and a few others were working hard to put together the best techniques and training possible for their children. With hard work, as well as trial and error, they hoped to give their children mostly normal lives.

Unlike what many of them had endured.

Hayla stirred, moving her lips. Fatherhood was still new, but even Thorin could tell his daughter would soon be hungry.

Thorin finally spoke aloud again. "All I want for

our daughters is for them to enjoy their childhood, something neither of us had the chance to do. Me being half-Brevkan, and you being royalty, we had to grow up far too quickly."

Kason murmured, "Yes, we agree on that. Although I would add that their safety is another important concern."

He finally looked away from his tiny daughter to Kason's face. The prince was notorious about giving him a hard time, and they had an unspoken agreement to avoid talking about emotions or anything too sensitive. While they weren't enemies, there were many reasons they would never be close friends. Kason was the leader of the Kelderan colony and couldn't show impartiality. Or, at least he tried not to do so in public.

Kason's human bride, Taryn, walked over to them, a slightly older baby asleep on her shoulder. Her Kelderan was improving, but still not perfect. "You two are serious. What are you planning?"

The prince switched to CEL—the human language—and Thorin went back to staring at his daughter. While Hayla had his black hair, everything else was from Vala—the golden skin, small nose, and even the shapes of the faint outlines of her markings.

She was perfect. More than that, holding her created a sense of peace Thorin had never known.

He would die protecting his little daughter.

Vala's whisper filled his ear. "You're making the

face again, the serious one, as if you're planning out her entire life in detail."

He smiled at Vala. "I'm only up to two years old. Give me a month, and I'll devise the rest."

She laughed. Leaning against his side, Vala stared at Hayla, too. "Just leave a little room for her to discover who she is, *zylar*. That way, she doesn't have to wait as long as we did to find happiness."

After kissing the top of Vala's head, he leaned his cheek against her hair and they both smiled down at their daughter. With his bride at his side and his daughter in his arms, Thorin had never been happier. Although it if were up to him, he'd work tirelessly to make them all a little happier each and every day.

**Ready for Kajala to find her happy ending?
Keep reading for an excerpt from:**

The Survivor
Kelderan Runic Warriors #6

About a year ago, Davrel Kolari was captured by a cruel pirate gang called the Rovers. They cut off his arm, turned him into one of their slaves, and made his life hell. Only because he learns how the Rovers want to assassinate the entire Kelderan royal family —including the female he intended to marry—does he fight to live and find a way to escape. His plan is to warn his old trainer and former general of the danger, extract a promise from them to protect his ex-love, and then let them do what they will with him.

Kajala Mayven has adjusted to being a single mother and living on a distant planet. With her son as her top priority, she cements some plans for her future and does her best to make them a reality. But then her former lover and father of her child suddenly reappears out of nowhere, a shadow of the male he once was, adamant about pushing her away. However, Kajala isn't about to give up so easily and is determined to help him heal for the sake of her son.

As the pair learn about how they've each changed, they both realize that maybe they fit together better now than before. However, unless they can destroy the pirate gang looking for Davrel, they'll never have a happy future. Will they find a way to destroy the Rovers? Or, will Davrel have to give up everything again to protect his female and baby son?

Chapter One

Nearly One Year Ago, In Deep Space

Davrel Kolari checked his console again to ensure the sensor jamming device was still engaged and blocking the enemy's scanners.

Yes. All was still functioning, meaning the space pirates couldn't tell exactly what his ship was up to, let alone that he was the only one still on board.

He wouldn't be able to escape in time, but that wasn't the plan. He just needed a minute or so more to save the others. And given how damaged the Kelderan ship was from the pirates' initial attack, it was a miracle he'd been able to divert power to keep the jamming device running this long.

His fingers flew across the console, looking for the quickest way to erase the ship's computer. Davrel was good with computers, but the latest

Kelderan spaceship was the most advanced to date, and even he needed some extra time to get anything done.

As a warning flashed on his screen about the precious power supply running low, he moved his head to another screen to check the status of the Kelderan escape pods. They would be at the necessary, safe distance in three...two...one.

Good, they'll make it. His crewmates would now be within teleportation range of another Kelderan ship, meaning the space pirates couldn't capture them.

Now it was time for phase two of his plan—to deny the pirates what they really wanted: the spaceship.

Davrel quickly brought up a different screen and tried to type in the self-destruct code. The only way to protect his people back on Keldera was to keep the knowledge from the Rover space pirates. Because if the bastards captured the ship—the most advanced of the entire Kelderan fleet—they'd sell it to the highest bidder, revealing all of their latest technological advancements. It would give an enemy a powerful heads-up over how to attack the Kelderans where it hurt the most.

How anyone had found out about the top-secret maiden voyage of their fastest, most advanced ship, he had no idea.

But if Davrel didn't protect the secrets of his planet, it would put everyone at risk.

Which meant it would put the love of his life at risk too.

Trying not to think about Kajala and how he'd never be able to follow through and honorably take her as his bride, Davrel focused on giving her a future. Maybe if she learned about what he'd done, she'd find a way to forgive him.

Especially considering he'd been weak and had claimed her before marrying her. He only hoped she didn't carry their child, or she would truly go through hell.

Stop it, Dav. Saving her and the planet is more important.

He finished typing in the correct self-destruct sequence with fifteen seconds to spare. However, nothing happened. No countdown, no acknowledgment of initiation, nothing but a blinking cursor on the screen.

And since he'd had to disable the voice activation commands to conserve energy, the only way to manually self-destruct the ship was to go to the main engineering room.

Just as the jamming device failed, he ran out of the main command deck and down the hall toward the main engineering access point.

He ran inside and skidded to a halt next to the heart of the ship's computer. Since manually initiating the self-destruct mechanism would take time—maybe too much time—he first typed the code to wipe all computer information databases. As the screen whirled to delete files, he ran to a panel on the side of the room, one covered in glass.

Davrel pressed his thumb to the reader, and it unlocked the glass. After opening it, he faced a row of three levers. Each one had to be engaged in a certain way before the ship self-destructed. The protocol was in place to prevent any mistakes or accidents.

He reached the first lever, typed in the necessary code, and slowly turned it, grunting at the effort. The more he turned it, the more his heart thundered in his chest. Funny to think he, the son of a pair of specialty merchants, was in charge of trying to protect his entire planet from who knew how many potential enemies. But if he wanted to save everyone he loved, the pirates couldn't get this ship, no matter what.

Once the first switch clicked in place, he moved to the second one and repeated the process, keeping his ears open for any invaders. The band of space pirates who'd discovered them had teleportation capabilities, which meant they should be on board now that the jamming devices were down.

They could locate him at any second. Only because the new Kelderan ship was over a mile long did Davrel have any chance at successfully detonating the ship in time. Provided it took his enemies too long to find him, of course.

The second lever also clicked into place and he

moved to the final one as sweat dripped down his brow. He knew he had to do this—and would do this —but he was seconds away from dying.

Dying and never seeing the beautiful smile of his love, never discussing complex engineering ideas with her, never holding her warm, naked body against his.

I'm doing this for you, Jala. I hope you know that. I love you.

Swallowing, Davrel kept the image of Kajala in his mind as he began turning the third lever.

He was about a quarter of the way done when an unknown voice spoke. He didn't understand the language but had a feeling he knew what they were demanding—stop, or they'd kill him.

He turned the lever some more, hoping he could finish before they tried. Just another small turn should set off the detonation.

Hot, excruciating pain coursed through his arm as a bright, burning light flashed quickly through it. He barely had a chance to register that his arm lay on the ground, separated from his body, before darkness consumed him.

About the Author

Jessie Donovan has sold over half a million books, has given away hundreds of thousands more to readers for free, and has even hit the *NY Times* and *USA Today* bestseller lists. She is best known for her dragon-shifter series, but also writes about magic users, aliens, and even has a crazy romantic comedy series set in Scotland. When not reading a book, attempting to tame her yard, or traipsing around some foreign country on a shoestring, she can often be found interacting with her readers on Facebook. She lives near Seattle, where, yes, it rains a lot but it also makes everything green.

Visit her website at: www.JessieDonovan.com